W9-BOA-229

Text and illustrations copyright © 2022 by Anne Yvonne Gilbert
Edited by Amy Novesky and Kate Riggs / Designed by Rita Marshall
Published in 2022 by Creative Editions / P.O. Box 227, Mankato, MN 56002 USA
Creative Editions is an imprint of The Creative Company / www.thecreativecompany.us
Library of Congress Cataloging-in-Publication Data
Names: Gilbert, Anne Yvonne, author, illustrator. Title: The red canoe / by Anne Yvonne Gilbert.
Summary: As an abandoned canoe reminisces about bygone adventures with its beloved boy, are
the best days behind it—or is there a glimmer of new life just ahead? Identifiers: LCCN 2021012003 /
ISBN 978-1-56846-368-1 Subjects: CYAC: Canoes and canoeing—Fiction. / Change—Fiction.
Classification: LCC PZ7.1.G5515 Re 2022   DDC [E]—dc23
First edition 9 8 7 6 5 4 3 2 1

THE RED CANOE

ANNE YVONNE GILBERT

CREATIVE EDITIONS

THE

old boathouse stood in the weak winter sun, its wooden sides creaking and groaning in the cold air. Slivers of light slipped through its missing planks and lit on the swirling dust and shrouded shapes lying in its shadows.

WRAPPED

in stiff canvas like an ancient mummy
lay the old red canoe, its fragile ribs
grown brittle with age, its once bright
paint faded, forgotten.

Generations of mice had nibbled holes
in its canvas sides, while a family of
raccoons had taken up residence, its
hull providing shelter and warmth.

TIME

moved slowly, and yet it was winter again, and the red canoe remembered . . .

The summer day, long ago, when it left the place where it was built, brand-new, its glossy red sides gleaming in the sun, and arrived at the house by the lake.

The boy with the big smile on his face who couldn't wait for the red canoe to be placed in the water before he jumped up into it.

THE

red canoe loved his boy. They launched
into the lake together that first day and
every summer day after that, the canoe
wondering at the ripple of cool water
against its sides and the weight of the
boy balancing in its bows.

TOGETHER

they discovered the water, how it
rocked them gently, then bounced and
splashed down the tumbling creeks,
sending them rushing through the
rocks. They learned of its strength as
it pushed back against their paddles or
lifted them effortlessly on a wave, and
that it had moods that depended on
the weather.

THEY

explored the rippling, deep-green lake,
finding all its hidden bays and shores
and laying claim to each one. They
built camps and lit fires, and on warm
nights laid a bed beneath the stars.

THEY

received the secrets of the woods and
waterways—where the beaver built its
lodge and how many kits were born,
where the moose brought its calf down
to drink in the cool evenings, and
where the heron liked to dive. They
found the best spot to fish, drifting
dreamily under cloudless skies.

How lucky they were.

EVERY

summer the boy got bigger and stronger, his limbs sturdier, his head more level, and he and the red canoe traveled farther and farther, its belly packed with supplies. They learned to portage between the lakes and navigate long distances by compass and stars.

EACH

fall the boy lovingly cleaned and repaired

the red canoe. Then, carefully, he wrapped

it in soft, dry canvas, tucking in the corners

and making it tight. Snug and safe in the

boathouse, the red canoe would dream

away the winters.

AND

each spring the doors of the boathouse would open, and the boy would carry the red canoe into the warm sun, remove its canvas cover, and wake it from its long sleep.

It should have gone on forever. But one year, news from abroad left the boy restless. A war was being fought in faraway lands. The boy could not roam and fish when others his age were marching into battle, bravely laying down their lives. So he went.

THE

red canoe waited for the boy to return. Waited for the spring day when the doors would open and the boy would carry him out into the sunshine once more.

The red canoe waited a long time. Summer turned into winter, again and again. So many winters, and the world was changing in so many ways. The red canoe was changing, too.

THE

lake and the forest continued the
endless cycle of birth and rebirth,
while inside, the canoe slept on, the
dust settling on its painted skin and
mice making nests in its ribs. The
old boathouse offered almost no pro-
tection against the ice and snow, and
the canoe felt its life drifting away, its
memories so old and faded they barely
existed. Patiently it had braced its old
cedar hull against cold and decay, the
sharp little teeth, the clambering paws.

IT

could barely remember the boy's smiling
face and the green waters of the lake.

The red canoe lay as cold as a stone,
when the boathouse door opened,
creaking loudly on its rusty hinges.

A BOY

shouted, "Look! It's a canoe!" and the red canoe was lifted out into the light and felt the warmth of sunshine and little hands touching its side.

It was summer once again.